001010302

Jackson County Library System
Medford, OR 97501

SHADY COVE

D0432048

RECEIVED MAR 0 7 1996

Date Due

JAN 2 8 '97			
APR 3 0 199			
MAY 19 '98			
NOV 13 '98			
DEC 31 '98			
AUG 13 '00			
SEP 30 '01			
AUG 29 '01			
APR 13 0			
SEP 07 '05			
MAR 15 06			

WITHDRAWN
Damaged, Obsolete, or Surplus

Jackson County Library Services

Jackson
County
Library
Services

HEADQUARTERS
413 W.Main
Medford, Oregon 97501

Connie Came to play

Jill Paton Walsh
Illustrated by Stephen Lambert

Viking

JACKSON COUNTY LIBRARY SYSTEM
MEDFORD, OREGON 97501

VIKING

Published by the Penguin Group
Penguin Books Ltd, 27 Wrights Lane, London W8 5TZ, England
Penguin Books USA Inc., 375 Hudson Street, New York, New York 10014, USA
Penguin Books Australia Ltd, Ringwood, Victoria, Australia
Penguin Books Canada Ltd, 10 Alcorn Avenue, Toronto, Ontario, Canada M4V 3B2
Penguin Books (NZ) Ltd, 182–190 Wairau Road, Auckland 10, New Zealand

Penguin Books Ltd, Registered Offices: Harmondsworth, Middlesex, England

First published 1995
1 3 5 7 9 10 8 6 4 2

Text copyright © Jill Paton Walsh, 1995
Illustrations copyright © Stephen Lambert, 1995

The moral right of the author and illustrator has been asserted

All rights reserved. Without limiting the rights under copyright reserved above, no part
of this publication may be reproduced, stored in or introduced into a retrieval system,
or transmitted, in any form or by any means (electronic, mechanical, photocopying,
recording or otherwise), without the prior written permission of both the copyright owner
and the above publisher of this book

A CIP catalogue record for this book is available from the British Library

ISBN 0–670–86210–X

When Connie came to play in Robert's house . . .

. . . Robert was cross.
"This is *my* train!" he said.

"All right," said Connie.
"You play with that one. I'll play with this one . . ."

"This is *my* rope!" said Robert.

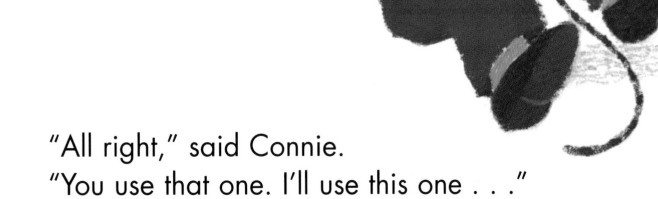

"All right," said Connie.
"You use that one. I'll use this one . . ."

"This is *my* trumpet!" said Robert.

"All right," said Connie.
"You blow that one. I'll blow this one . . ."

"This is *my* horse!" said Robert.

"All right," said Connie.
"You ride that one. I'll ride this one . . ."

"This is *my* diving set!" said Robert.

"All right," said Connie.
"You swim like that. I'll swim like this . . ."

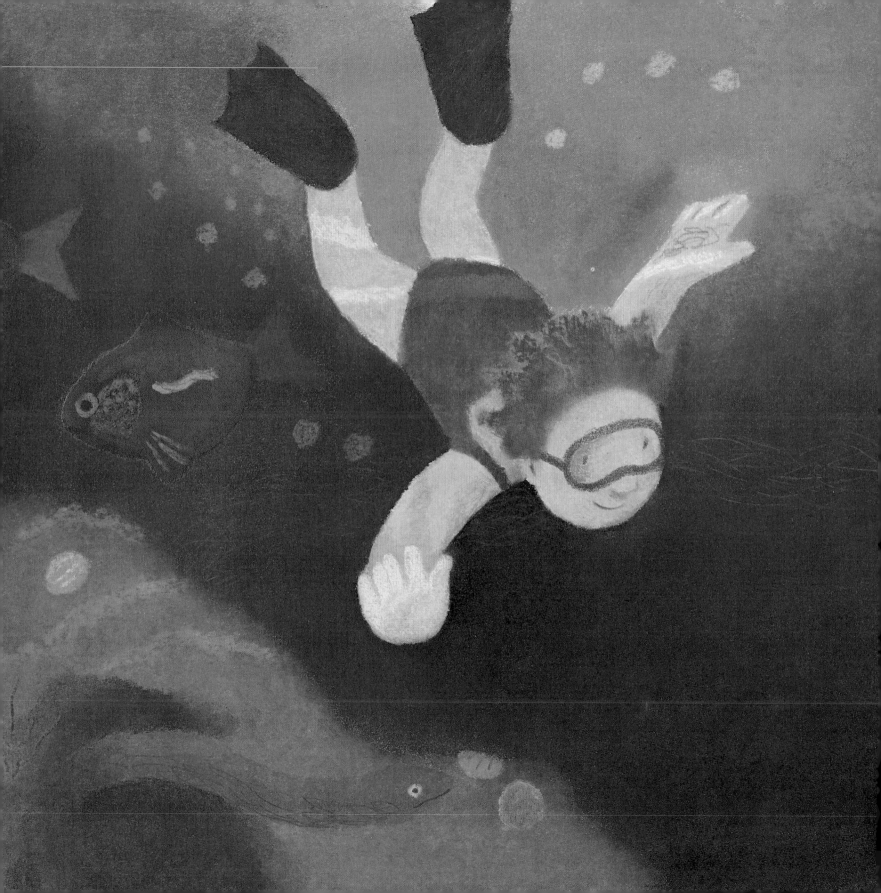

"These are *my* bricks!" said Robert.

"All right," said Connie.
"You build with those. I'll build with these . . ."

"Everything is mine," said Robert.
"All right," said Connie. "I'll play in my head."
"You can't share with me, then," said Robert.

"Yes I can," Connie said. "I can tell you a story . . ."

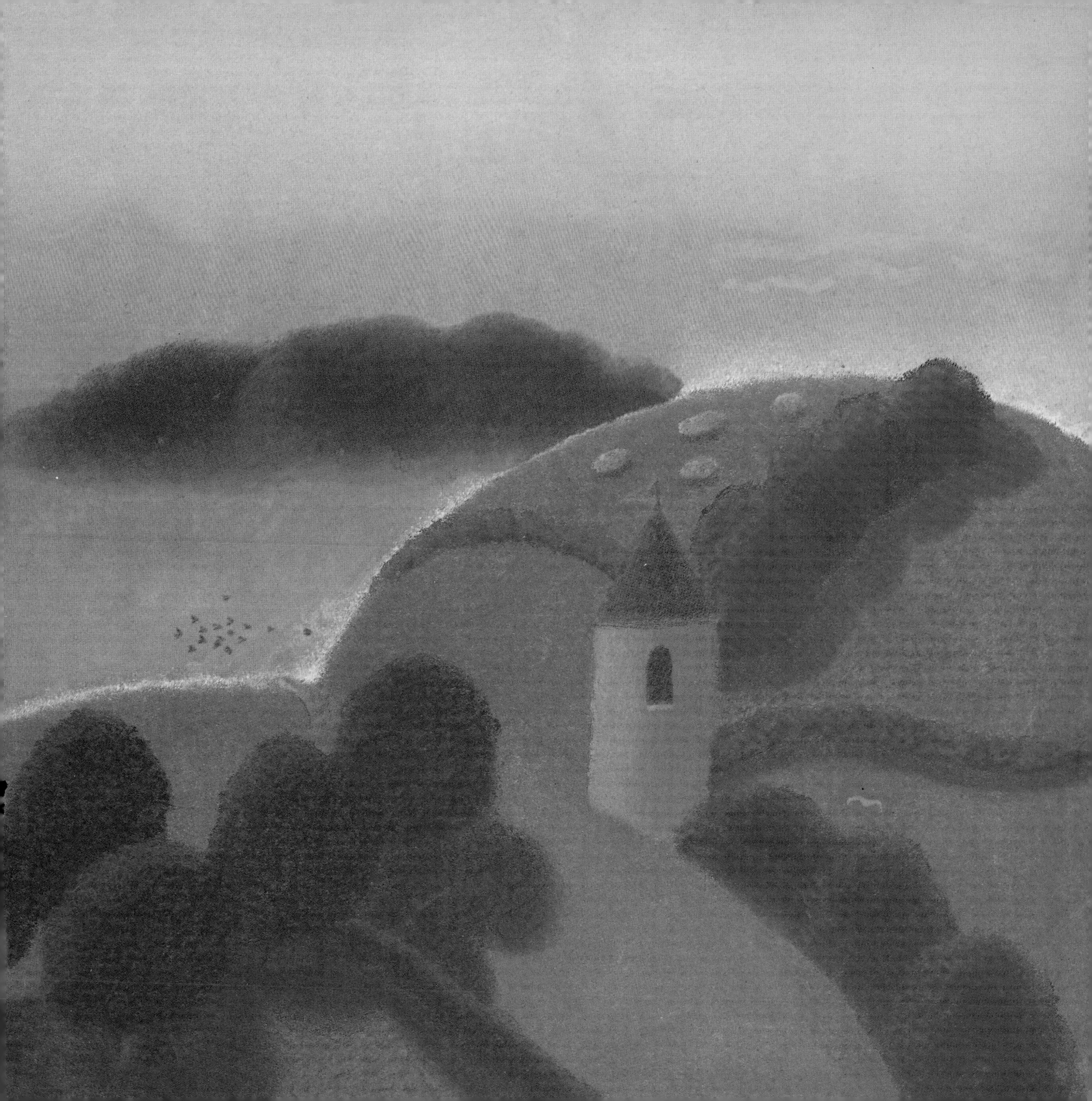